GUINEA PIG KILLER

THE NIGHTMARE CLUB

GUINEA PIG KILLER

BY

ANNIE GRAVES

ILLUSTRATED BY

GLENN McELHINNEY

darbycreek

MINNEAPOLIS

Darby Creek
A division of Lerner Publishing Group, Inc.
241 First Avenue North
Minneapolis, MN 55401 USA

For reading levels and more information, look up this title
at www.lernerbooks.com.

Main body text set in ITC Stone Serif Std., 11.5/15.
Typeface provided by Adobe Systems.

Library of Congress Cataloging-in-Publication Data

Graves, Annie.
    Guinea pig killer / by Annie Graves ; illustrated by
Glenn McElhinney.
        pages   cm. — (The Nightmare Club)
    Originally published: Dublin, Ireland : Little Island,
2011.
    ISBN 978–1–4677–4351–8 (lib. bdg. : alk. paper)
    ISBN 978–1–4677–7637–0 (eBook)
    [1. Guinea pigs—Fiction. 2. Ghosts—Fiction.
3. Brothers and sisters—Fiction. 4. Horror stories.]
I. McElhinney, Glenn, illustrator. II. Title.
PZ7.G77512Gui 2015
[Fic]—dc23   2014015299

Manufactured in the United States of America
1 – SB – 12/31/14

*For Much Misunderstood,
the most beautiful toad in the world*

Annie Graves is twelve years old, and she has no intention of ever growing up. She is, conveniently, an orphan, and lives at an undisclosed address in the Glasnevin area of Dublin, Ireland, with her pet toad, Much Misunderstood, and a small black kitten, Hugh Shalby Nameless. You needn't think she goes to school—pah!—or has anything as dull as brothers and sisters or hobbies, but let's just say she keeps a large cauldron on the stove.

This is not her first book. She has written eight so far, none of which is her first.

Publisher's note: We did try to take a picture of Annie, but her face just kept fading away. We have sent our camera for investigation but suspect the worst.

THANK you!

I'd better thank Deirdre Sullivan for her help with this book, or she might unleash her ungrateful guinea pig on me while she smiles evilly and eats cake.

This is me, Annie Graves, author extraordinaire. (That's French, not a spelling mistake.)

Look, just so you know, this whole Nightmare Club thing was my idea. Because having a nightmare by yourself is kinda scary. But kids sharing their nightmares at a sleepover on Halloween night, when the grown-ups are not around and that spooky knocking from the basement . . . just . . . WON'T . . . stop. That's really DEAD scary.

Which is why I call it the Nightmare Club.

Everyone has to tell a story. That's how the Nightmare Club works. And it'd better be a scary one, or you're out. Home you go. One year we made Harold ring his uncle, Mr. Crosse, to come and get him.

That was because he told a stupid story. It was about a bat that couldn't find its belfry or some rubbish like that. Everyone knows bats don't really live in belfries. They live right in your own attic. And they swoop down in the night and scrabble about in your hair with their pinchy little claws...

So anyway, we sent Harold packing. Because only the scariest stories are good enough for the Nightmare Club.

That's my rule.

This is Kate's story.

She's a strange girl, Kate. But I suppose if your neighbor was being haunted by a guinea pig, you might turn a little bit odd yourself.

This isn't really my story,
Kate said.

It happened over the summer to a neighbor of mine called Sandy. But I'm going to tell it anyway.

Sandy had a
sister called
Dolly.

She was a
teenager.

She didn't
really want to
be hanging out
with us kids.

She was boring anyway.

All she cared about was school and people
she knew from school and what they said
and what they did and who they were
annoyed at and why.

Though I suppose that wasn't
completely all.

You see, she had this guinea pig.

Princess Snowflake was the guinea pig's name, and Dolly loved her more than anything else in the world.

When Dolly was sad, she would take the little princess out of her cage and tell her all about her problems.

She would scratch the guinea pig's soft white fur until Princess Snowflake made deep, happy noises.

Sandy was jealous of Her Royal Highness.

That is not how he would see it, of course.

He would just say the guinea pig was gross
and boring.

Well, I suppose if I had a sister and she
preferred an animal that sometimes ate its
own poo, then I would be a little put out
as well.

Anyway, time came and went, and over
the summer Sandy's family all went away.

Mr. and Mrs. Mount went on holiday.
They did that every year, without Sandy,
and he said it was very unfair.

He had to stay with us, and it rained and
rained all the time and we never got to
the beach, even for one day.

Sandy's sister wasn't on holiday with their parents, though. She was studying abroad.

And she had left very strict instructions for Sandy about how he was supposed to look after her beloved guinea pig while she was away.

Feed her
Cuddle her
Brush her
Fresh water
Change the hay
(Look after her or else!)
Dolly xxx

He was supposed to go home every day and feed Princess Snowflake and make sure she was all right.

We didn't know this.

We'd forgotten all about the wretched guinea pig. She wasn't in our house, so we never gave her a thought.

Now, Sandy was pretty bitter about being abandoned by his family.

The way he thought about it, it was all Princess Snowflake's fault.

If she wasn't around, he reasoned, he wouldn't have to stay home and mind her and feed her and change her hay and all that stuff.

He would be able to go on holiday with
his parents and not have to stay with
a silly girl (me) in a house that smelled
funny.

(My house doesn't smell funny at all,
but it does smell different from Sandy's
house because Sandy's house has a weird,
mustardy smell that I don't like very
much.)

Anyway, he was wrong to blame Princess Snowflake, because she was only a guinea pig.

What could she do about it? Make Sandy's parents take him with them on holiday? I don't think so.

I mean, her favorite treat was cabbage
leaves, and she hid under her bedding
whenever the television was turned up
too loud.

How much more harmless can you get?

I still don't know if Sandy did what he did
to that poor animal on purpose or not.

But this is what he did.

He stayed with us all that time, and he
never said he was supposed to go home
every day and feed her.

Not until the day before his parents came
back from their cruise.

And by then, of course, Her Highness was already dead.

He called me over to the house to show me the body.

He wasn't sad at all, just worried that he would get into trouble.

The cage door was all nibbled, as if she'd tried to escape.

Her bowl was empty and dry as bones.

I had never seen a dead body before, and it was all stiff and pointy.

Her long white teeth were bared, as if she had been just about to bite or let out a guinea pig scream.

Sandy put the body in the trash, and I
went home angry.

I didn't speak to him for ages after that.

I kept thinking about my little black puppy, Rock. His big, soft eyes and snuffly coal-black nose.

What if someday I had to go study abroad and somebody "forgot" about him?

Thinking about it made my eyes all sting-y.

So that was why I didn't really get the chance to see what happened afterward for myself.

All I know is what Sandy told me later, when I felt too sorry for him to stay mad.

After Sandy's parents got back from their trip, they were very angry with him.

He was in a lot of trouble.

But they decided not to tell Dolly what
had happened.

I suppose they thought that she would be
so sad and angry about what he did that
she might never speak to him ever again.

So what they did was this.

They decided to buy a replacement guinea
pig for Dolly, one that looked exactly like
Princess Snowflake, and to pretend that
none of it had ever happened.

Luckily, there was a guinea pig that looked exactly like Princess Snowflake in the first pet shop they visited.

She had been delivered that very morning.

Just left outside the pet shop in a little box.

It was the strangest thing, the shopkeeper said. The very strangest thing.

They took the new guinea pig home, and Sandy's parents stood over him as he fed and cared for it every single day.

It was a frightened little creature, but sometimes it stared at Sandy as if it hated him. As if it knew what he was—a guinea pig killer.

Now and then the new guinea pig would make little squeaking noises with pauses in between.

It sounded like it was talking to another guinea pig.

Of course, it wasn't doing any such thing. There was no one else there.

And no other guinea pig either.

Sandy began to have nightmares almost as soon as the new Princess Snowflake moved into their house.

SQUEAAK!!!

SQUEAAK!!

SQUEAAK!!!

In these dreams, he was moving through a strange, dark world.

The only things he could make out in the gloom were two bright red dots, moving slowly but steadily toward him.

He didn't want the dots to get to him, so he would try to hide from them.

They always found him, though, crouched behind a sofa or against the wall with a heavy curtain pulled around him.

It wasn't until the night before Dolly's return that he realized the dark place of his dreams was his own house.

That night the two red dots made their way to the door of his bedroom, and he was very glad to wake up before he could see what happened to him.

Dolly came home full of talk, and she didn't seem to notice anything wrong with Princess Snowflake.

Before he went to sleep that night, Sandy
pushed a chair, a toy box, and his bulging
laundry basket right against the door.

He dreamed of the two red dots swinging
like the pendulum on the hall clock.

Back and forth, back and forth. Harder
and faster, faster and harder.

So hard and fast that they should have
made a noise.

Only they didn't.

In this nightmare world you couldn't
make a noise.

Even when you tried to, no sound came.

But in the morning the toy box and the laundry basket were spilled out all over the floor.

Trucks and socks everywhere.

Dirty clothes all mingled with his teddies and Legos.

Sandy's mother made him tidy it all up.

Dolly helped him, though he kind of wished she wouldn't.

She kept going on about how good he was to take care of Princess Snowflake, even though he didn't like her as much as Dolly did.

Mixed in with the toys and clothes, Sandy
found a small brown bean.

At first he didn't know what it could be,
but then Dolly asked if Princess Snowflake
had been in his room.

And then he knew.

Later on, he stared at the hard brown lump sitting on top of the trash bag like the egg of a strange and disgusting bird.

It was the poo of a guinea pig, he knew that.

But which guinea pig?

And what did it mean?

That was the
night the rash
arrived.

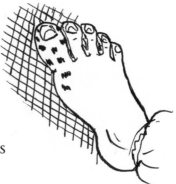

It started with
a dream where
something small and
cold kept pinching his
big toe.

Hard.

It hurt, and when he woke up
the pain was still there.

His big toe was covered in little red marks.

He scratched at the rash, but that only made it itchier.

His mother called it eczema.

She slathered it with cream that didn't do very much good.

Every night the rash spread farther and farther.

It was halfway up his leg by the time they went to the doctor.

The doctor said it didn't look like a normal rash; it looked like something was biting him.

There was a stronger cream to put on.

A green one this time.

It smelled like toilet cleaner and, after a while, so did Sandy.

Nobody wanted to sit beside him in school because the smell was so strong and he was always twitching and scratching.

His mother changed his bedsheets and cleaned his room from top to bottom.

They made him stop eating milk and cheese and chocolate, in case he was allergic to something.

And he had to wash with a special type of soap.

Meanwhile, the rash kept spreading and spreading and the dreams felt more and more real.

In his nightmares, the furry thing was on his tummy.

Its nose burrowed into the crook of his arm.

How could something so small be so heavy and so strong?

Sandy did ask his
mother one time
if she thought
it could be the
ghost of Princess
Snowflake
getting her
revenge.

But she told him
not to be silly.

He didn't feel
silly, though. He felt afraid.

When he closed his eyes, the two red dots
were there all the time now.

Even if he was awake.

The little red eyes.

On a living guinea pig, the eyes had
seemed so helpless.

They weren't helpless now.

They were angry.

Sandy had no idea what he could do to stop the eyes from troubling him, but he knew someone who might.

Dolly had been nice to Sandy since she came back.

She felt sorry for him, especially now that the rash was way up his face.

His mother was still making him put on that disgusting cream, even though it wasn't working.

So Dolly hung out with him, even though
he looked like he had freckles made of
scabs and would go pale whenever she
mentioned guinea pigs.

Sandy didn't want to tell her the truth.

He had to, though.

She had known Princess Snowflake (the first Princess Snowflake) better than anyone.

She might know how to stop whatever was happening to him.

It had to stop soon.

Sandy could not take much more of the nighttime nibbling.

Dolly sat and listened to the story without saying a word.

When Sandy was finished, she asked him why he would make up such a horrible lie.

You see, Dolly had painted the tiny toenails of Princess Snowflake with pink nail polish.

This way she could tell her apart from other guinea pigs that were white all over with big red eyes.

(And, well, it also looked adorable.)

When she had come home after studying abroad, the polish was still there, and so was the scar that Snowflake had gotten on her back that time the vet had to remove a lump.

It was definitely the same guinea pig.

Sandy didn't know what to say to that.

That night Princess Snowflake the Second disappeared.

The hutch was empty in the morning, and try as they might, they couldn't find the guinea pig anywhere.

The weird thing was, the hutch door was locked from the outside.

Dolly refused to speak to Sandy for six weeks.

She thought that his story from the day before was the start of some mean trick.

Six weeks
was also the
amount of time
it took for the rash
to fade.

Things are back to normal
now, except that Sandy is scared of
anything small and furry.

Once, he started to cry like a baby when I
threw a teddy bear at him.

Oh, and Rock is a lot bigger now, and I
haven't forgotten to feed him even once.

Even though his eyes are large and soft
and brown and could never haunt you in
your nightmares.

THE END

That story really spooked me.

I mean, it sounds kind of silly, doesn't it? A guinea pig ghost. But then you hear about those beady red eyes following people all over the place, and even if you snuggle right down under the covers you can still see them, staring right at you.

SHIIIIIVERS!

The only way to stop them is to hear another story ...